My Best Friend's Jesus

Author: Emerson H. "J.R." Stull

Illustrators: Allen M. Smallwood & Samantha J. Mellott

Editor: Sarah J. Smallwood

Arranged by: Jeannie M. Smallwood

 proving press

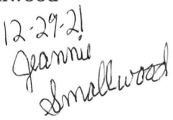

12-29-21
Jeannie
Smallwood

Book Design & Production: Columbus Publishing Lab
www.ColumbusPublishingLab.com

Paperback ISBN: 978-1-63337-518-5

Printed in the United States of America
1 3 5 7 9 10 8 6 4 2

This book has been published in remembrance and honor of J.R. Stull.

We dedicate this book to the friends and family of J.R., to the countless musicial artists that have touched his life, (too many to mention them all) and we give special mention to a few who J.R. considered good friends, that have impacted his life and his music.

Rhonda Vincent
An American Bluegrass singer, songwriter, and multi-instrumentalist.
Grammy Award Winner and inductee of the Grand Ole Opry

Rick Troyer
Owner, Manager and Instructor of Hummingbird Music Studio
(J.R.'s steel guitar instructor)

Marvin and Deana Clark
Founders of the Ohio Valley Opry.
(J.R. sang on their show a time or two and recorded
his last album at Clark Family Studio)

We also dedicate this book to the many lives that will be encountered by reading it and by the proceeds of it.

This book will be used in outreach ministry and given to children around the world. The proceeds from this book will be used to help young people learn to sing and play instruments.

This book is a song that J.R. wrote and is published in remembrance and honor of him by his family.

This song is about a poor kid
who's best friend is Jesus
Liza 7 years old

The song is kind of sad because the little boy is
made fun of, but happy because his friend is Jesus.
Addalyn 6 years old

I like this song because it's about Jesus.
Jesus died on the cross for us.
This book teaches us about kindness.
Lena 9 years old

You will never be alone.
You will always have a friend,
because Jesus will be your best friend.
Lily 11 years old

It was 9:00 am. the bell had rung.
The children were all in.

Your best friend...
why?

Prize

The teacher had a favorite game.
She called, "My Best Friend".

"You just stand and face the class,
tell them your best friend and why?

The one with the best reason,
well they'd receive a little prize."

Well the first to stand was Mary Ann.
She said, "My best friend is Sue,
because she always likes to do
the things I like to do".

John said his best friend was Bill,
of all the other boys,
cause he always shares his candy
and he always shares his toys.

There were many friends and many reasons,
that's to understand,
but Little Joe in the middle row
was holding up his hand.

Well the children laughed and made their fun,
   you know how children do.

The teacher finally calmed them down,
   when her little laugh was through
'cause they called him funny names
and told him Joe, "You never had a friend".

But a tear came into Joey's eye
when the teacher called on him.

Though his folks were poor
and his clothes were tore,
he stood up in the isle
and with his head held back
and shoulders high
he sang out with a smile.

"My best friend's Jesus, 'cause
He gives me the earth to walk upon.
He gives me food and drink
and the ability to think."

"My best friend's Jesus, cause
He's done more than anyone you see, 'cause
He suffered on the cross
and died for me."

The teacher hung her head in shame
as a tear came to her eye,
and all the children did the same.
Some of them even cried.

But there was no doubt in the teacher's mind
as to who would get the prize,
and when she handed Joe the bible,
Lord you should have seen his eyes.

Then he gave his song to Mrs. Jones
he said, "I wrote it too."

Well, she made a whole bunch of copies
and she passed them around the room.

The kids brought shoes and clothes to school
and Joey just felt like a king.

And every morning at 9:00 am
you can hear the 3rd grade sing.

My best friend's Jesus, cause
He gives me the earth to walk upon.
He gives me food and drink
and the ability to think.

My best friend's Jesus, cause
He's done more than anyone you see,
cause he suffered on the cross
and died for me.

The End

J.R. was known for his sense of humor, and what we call "J.R. ism"

"What have you been up to?"
"Oh everstuff."

"How are you doing?"
"Fantastic. I don't go any lower than fantastic."

"How do you feel today?"
"With my fingers."

"Hey, J.R. How are you?"
"I'm finer than a frog hair"
or "I'm just perfect but I'm getting better."

"It only hurts when you laugh."

"He Often said "Thanks for making my day special".

My Best Friend's Jesus is on the album
He Still Loves You, where J.R. gives thanks to his
Lord and Savior, Jesus Christ, for His inspiration,
words, and music to make the album possible.

He left his listeners with this encouragement...

**"Just remember,
no matter what's in your past
or how hard life gets,
He still loves you
even when you're not loveable!"**

**Very much love,
God bless,
J.R.**

CPSIA information can be obtained
at www.ICGtesting.com
Printed in the USA
LVHW070811301121
704794LV00003B/52